School Buses

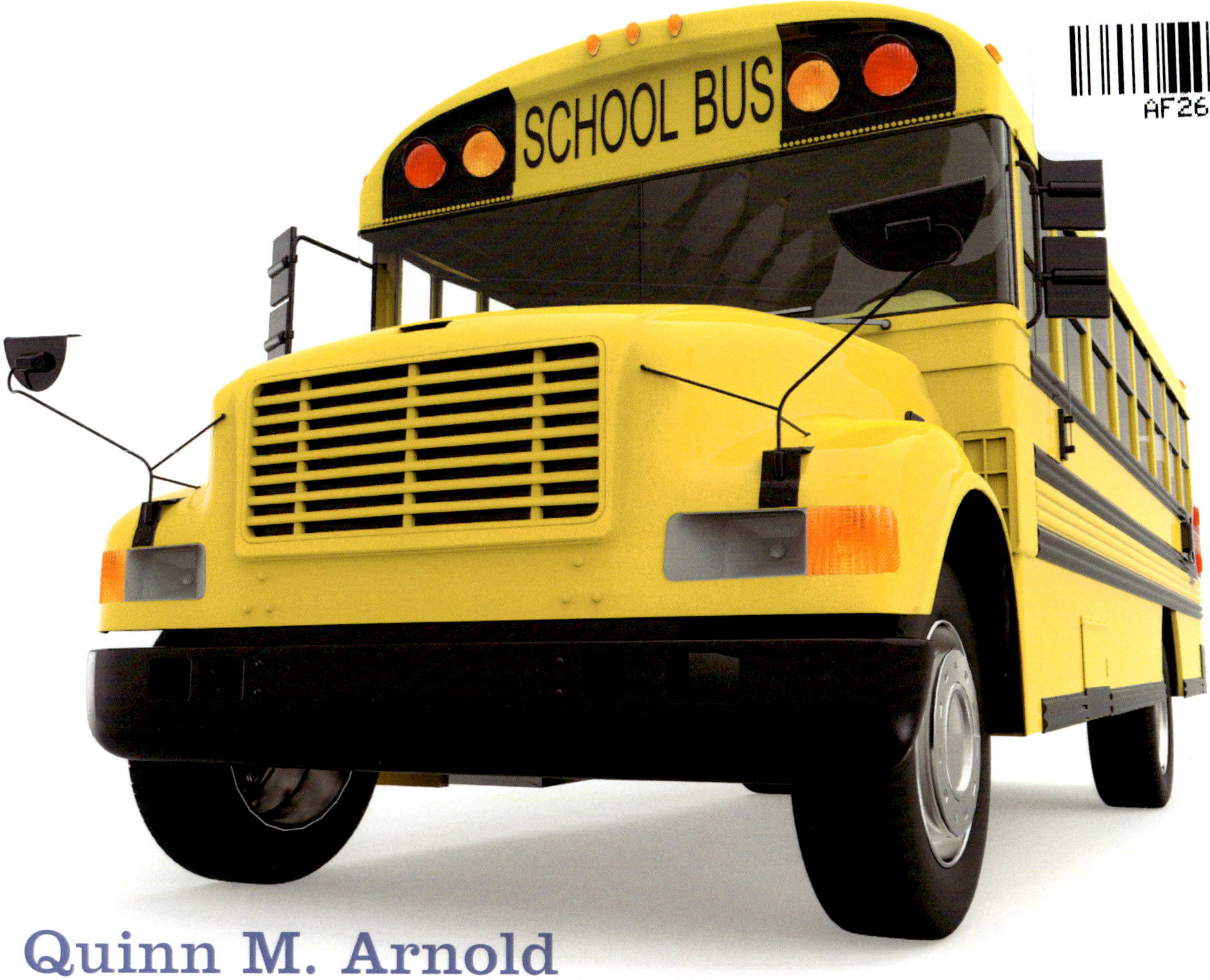

Quinn M. Arnold

seedlings

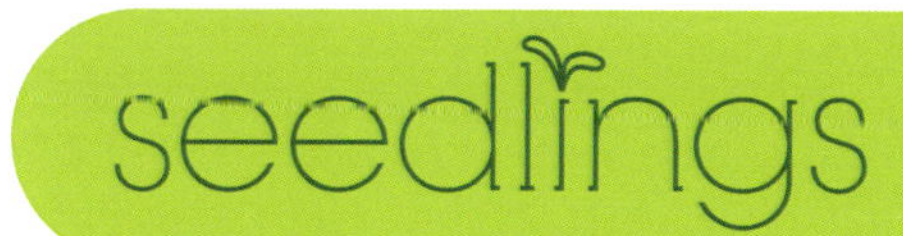

CREATIVE EDUCATION • CREATIVE PAPERBACKS

Published by Creative Education and Creative Paperbacks
P.O. Box 227, Mankato, Minnesota 56002
Creative Education and Creative Paperbacks are imprints of
The Creative Company
www.thecreativecompany.us

Design by Ellen Huber; production by Dana Cheit
Art direction by Rita Marshall

Photographs by Dreamstime (Anatoliy Samara), iStockphoto
(alacatr, ArtBoyMB, BanksPhotos, chris-mueller,
DigtialStorm, FrankvandenBergh, Ignatiev, kenneth-cheung,
Kubrak78, lisegagne, MBPROJEKT_Maciej_Biedowski,
monkeybusinessimages, Nerthuz, pyzata, sihuo0860371,
StphaneLemire, suprun, Willowpix, wsfurlan), Shutterstock (Jaren
Jai Wicklund)

Library of Congress Cataloging-in-Publication Data
Names: Arnold, Quinn M., author.
Title: School buses / Quinn M. Arnold.
Series: Seedlings.
Includes bibliographical references and index.
Summary: A kindergarten-level introduction to school buses,
covering their purpose, parts, community role, and such
defining features as their stop signs.
Identifiers: ISBN 978-1-64026-070-2 (hardcover) / ISBN 978-1-
62832-658-1 (pbk) / ISBN 978-1-64000-186-2 (eBook)

This title has been submitted for CIP processing under LCCN
2018939107

CCSS: RI.K.1, 2, 3, 4, 5, 6, 7; RI.1.1, 2, 3, 4, 5, 6, 7; RF.K.1, 3; RF.1.1

TABLE OF CONTENTS

Hello, school buses!

SCHOOL BUS
SCHOOL BUS

School buses go around
neighborhoods.

They take students to and from schools.

Most school buses are yellow. They have black stripes on the sides.

Some have a
wheelchair lift.

School buses have flashing lights. A stop sign folds out.

Other vehicles stop. Kids cross the road.

A school bus driver opens the door. The driver keeps kids on the bus safe.

School buses are long vehicles. There are many seats in a school bus.

A rear door can be opened
in an **emergency**.

School buses pick up students. They drop them off for school and sports.

They take kids home.

Goodbye,
school buses!

Picture a School Bus

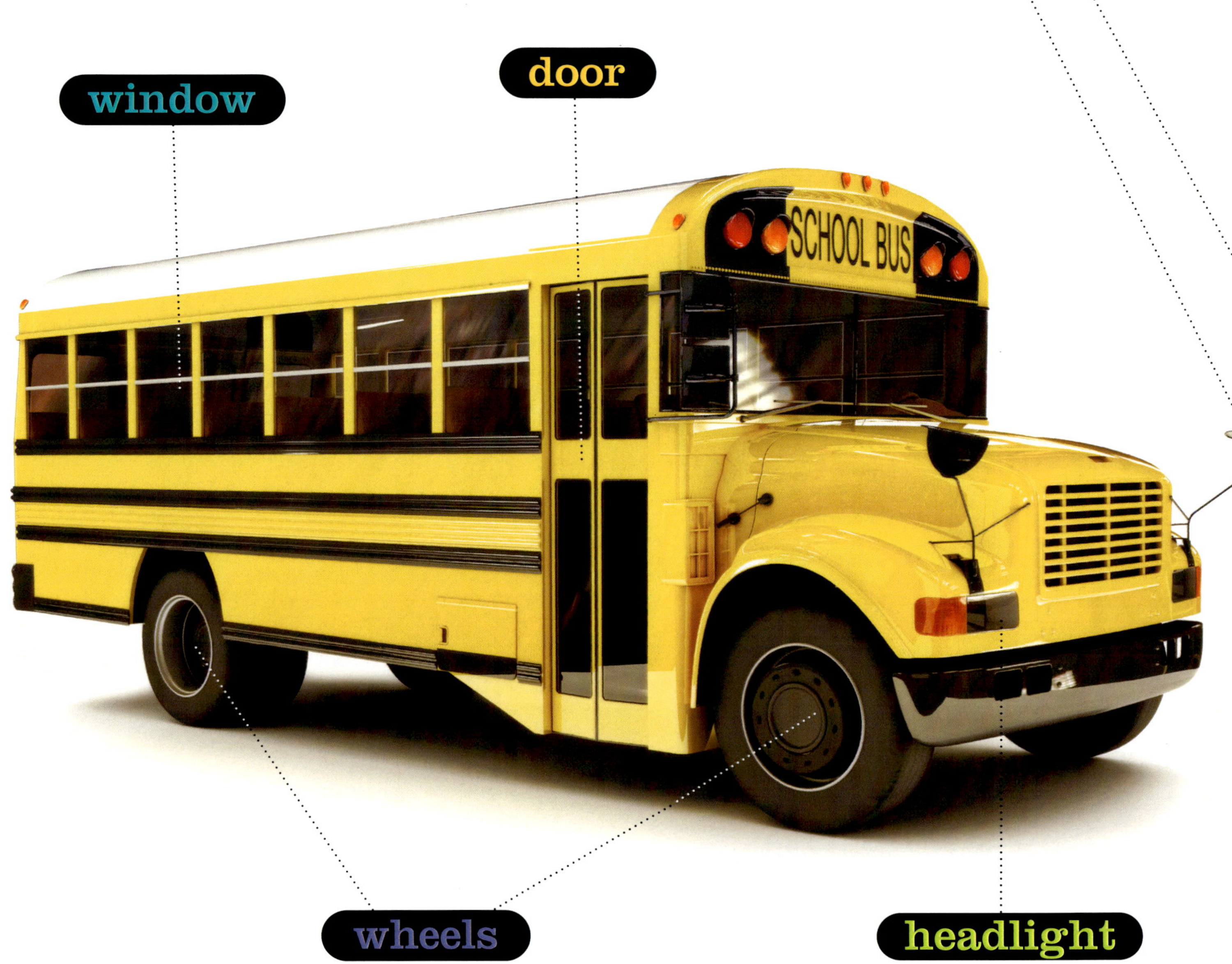

flashing lights

steering wheel

stop sign

bumper

emergency exit

emergency: something unexpected and often dangerous that happens suddenly

vehicles: machines such as cars or trucks that move people or things over land

wheelchair lift: a special machine that raises a person and their wheelchair up over steps

Morey, Allan. *School Buses.*
Minneapolis: Jump!, 2015.

Reinke, Beth Bence. *School Buses on the Go.*
Minneapolis: Lerner, 2018.

Easy School Bus Craft
https://happyhomefairy.com/easy-school-bus-craft/
Make your own school bus picture using construction paper
and paint.

Super Coloring: School Bus Coloring Pages
http://www.supercoloring.com/coloring-pages/transport
/school-bus
Print off a picture of a school bus to color.

Index